Note to parents, carers and teachers

Read it yourself is a series of modern stories, favourite characters and traditional tales written in a simple way for children who are learning to read. The books can be read independently or as part of a guided reading session.

Each book is carefully structured to include many high-frequency words vital for first reading. The sentences on each page are supported closely by pictures to help with understanding, and to offer lively details to talk about.

The books are graded into four levels that progressively introduce wider vocabulary and longer stories as a reader's ability and confidence grows.

Ideas for use

- Begin by looking through the book and talking about the pictures. Has your child heard this story before?

- Help your child with any words he does not know, either by helping him to sound them out or supplying them yourself.

- Developing readers can be concentrating so hard on the words that they sometimes don't fully grasp the meaning of what they're reading. Answering the puzzle questions on pages 30 and 31 will help with understanding.

For more information and advice on Read it yourself and book banding, visit **www.ladybird.com/readityourself**

Book Band 4

Level 1 is ideal for children who have received some initial reading instruction. Each story is told very simply, using a small number of frequently repeated words.

Special features:

Opening pages introduce key story words

The queen put a pea on the bed.

Next, she put a mattress on the pea.

Large, clear type

Careful match between story and pictures

Educational Consultant: Geraldine Taylor
Book Banding Consultant: Kate Ruttle

A catalogue record for this book is available from the British Library

Published by Ladybird Books Ltd
80 Strand, London, WC2R ORL
A Penguin Company

002

ISBN: 978-0-72327-514-5

Printed in China

The Princess
and the Pea

Illustrated by
Marie-Anne Didierjean

pea

prince   queen

princess

mattress

bed

Once there was a prince.

"I will only marry a real princess," said the prince.

"Is she a real princess?"
said the prince.

"No," said the queen.
"That girl is not
a real princess."

"Is she a real princess?"
said the prince.

"No," said the queen.
"That girl is not
a real princess."

One day, another girl
went to see the prince.

"Is she a real princess?"
said the prince. "I hope
she is."

"We will see," said
the queen.

The queen put a pea
on the bed.

Next, she put a mattress
on the pea.

The queen put another mattress on the bed.

She put on another mattress, and another and another.

The girl went to bed.

The next day, the queen
said, "Did you sleep well?"

"No," said the girl,
"I did not sleep well.
There was a pea in
the bed."

"Is she a real princess?"
said the prince.

"Yes!" said the queen.
"She is a real princess."

"Will you marry me?"
said the prince. "I hope
you will."

"Yes," said the girl.
"But only if you are
a real prince!"

How much do you remember about the story of The Princess and the Pea? Answer these questions and find out!

- Who does the prince want to marry?

- What does the queen put on the bed?

- What does she put on top of the pea?

Look at the pictures from the story and say the order they should go in.

A

B

C

D

Answer: B, D, A, C.

Read it yourself with Ladybird

Tick the books you've read!

Level 1

For children who are ready to take their first steps in reading.

Level 2

For beginner readers who can read short, simple sentences with help.